ROSALIND KERVEN trained as an anthropologist and is now a well-known children's editor, reviewer and author. Her most recent retellings of myths and legends include *The Mythical Quest* and *The Giant King: Looking at Norse Myth* (both The British Library), *Aladdin and Other Tales from the Arabian Nights* and *Tales from King Arthur* (both Dorling Kindersley). Her children's novel *The Sea is Singing* was chosen as a Times Education Supplement Book of the Year and dramatised for radio, while *Who Ever heard of a Vegetarian Fox?* was shortlisted for the Children's Book Award and selected for the Japanese Junior High School Reading List. Rosalind lives in Northumberland with her husband and two daughters.

ALAN MARKS took his degree in graphic design at Bath Academy and has since illustrated over 30 children's books. His first book, Storm, written by Kevin Crossley Holland, won the 1992 Carnegie Medal, *Ring a Ring o'Roses* the 1992 Bologna UNICEF Award, and *Over the Hills and Far Away* the U.S. NAPPA Silver Medal and Parents' Choice Illustration Award in 1994. In 1995 *The Thief's Daughter* became National Curriculum recommended reading, and in 1996 *Thomas and the Tinners* was a category winner of the Smarties Prize. Alan Marks is married with two daughters and lives in Kent.

This retelling is based on a traditional Scottish folk tale, which can be found in *Scottish Folk and Fairy Tales*, edited by Gordon Jarvis (Puffin, 1992).

First published in Great Britain in 1999 by
Frances Lincoln Limited, 4 Torriano Mews
Torriano Avenue, London NW5 2RZ

First paperback edition 2000

British Library Cataloguing in Publication Data
available on request

ISBN 0-7112-1352-6
ISBN 0-7112-1527-8

Set in Joanna MT

Printed in Hong Kong
1 3 5 7 9 8 6 4 2

THE
ENCHANTED
FOREST

A Scottish Fairy Tale

Rosalind Kerven
Illustrated by Alan Marks

FRANCES LINCOLN

Once upon a time there was a thick forest that was said to be enchanted. It was full of sweet, dark smells and very old, very beautiful. But nobody with any sense ever went inside it.

Nearby there lived a wild sort of girl called Janna. Her father owned all the land where the enchanted forest grew.

One day, when no one was looking, Janna climbed over a wall, squeezed under a fence and ran until she came to the forest edge.

Then she took a deep breath and went in.

Under the trees, everything was utterly still, eerily silent. Slowly, Janna walked on.

At last she came to an old well. Behind it, a lovely snow-white horse was standing, as if it were waiting for its rider.

Janna looked around. She couldn't see anyone. She called out, but nobody answered.

She crept closer to the well. The ancient bricks were half-hidden by a mass of fragrant wild roses. She reached out to pick one –

And in that instant ...

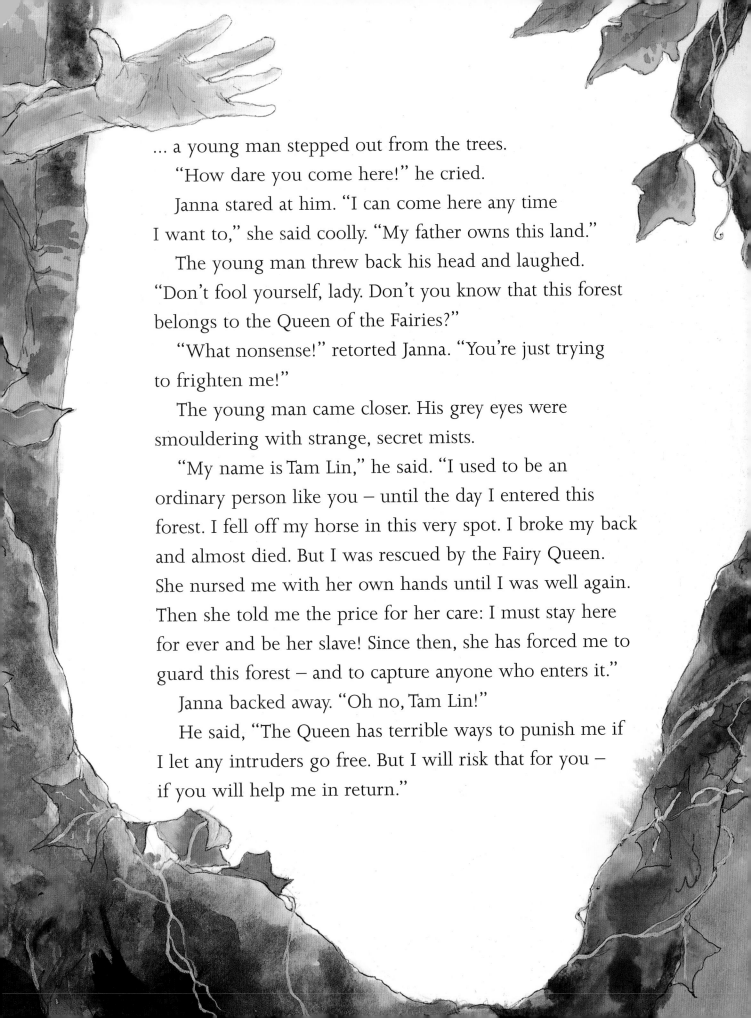

... a young man stepped out from the trees.

"How dare you come here!" he cried.

Janna stared at him. "I can come here any time
I want to," she said coolly. "My father owns this land."

The young man threw back his head and laughed.
"Don't fool yourself, lady. Don't you know that this forest
belongs to the Queen of the Fairies?"

"What nonsense!" retorted Janna. "You're just trying
to frighten me!"

The young man came closer. His grey eyes were
smouldering with strange, secret mists.

"My name is Tam Lin," he said. "I used to be an
ordinary person like you – until the day I entered this
forest. I fell off my horse in this very spot. I broke my back
and almost died. But I was rescued by the Fairy Queen.
She nursed me with her own hands until I was well again.
Then she told me the price for her care: I must stay here
for ever and be her slave! Since then, she has forced me to
guard this forest – and to capture anyone who enters it."

Janna backed away. "Oh no, Tam Lin!"

He said, "The Queen has terrible ways to punish me if
I let any intruders go free. But I will risk that for you –
if you will help me in return."

He seized her hand and led her back through shadowy paths to the forest edge. As she turned towards the sunlight, his grip suddenly tightened.

"You must come back here," he said, "at midnight tomorrow."

"But tomorrow is Hallowe'en!" cried Janna.

"And tomorrow," said Tam Lin, "the fairies' procession will pass by the well. I will be with them. You must watch for me – and pull me free!"

"But ..."

"The Fairy Queen will try to frighten you with her spells. But *do not let me go!* For nothing can hurt you if ..."

"If what, Tam Lin?"

"If you love me," he said.

And suddenly her hand was free, the trees swallowed him up, and he was gone.

The next night came: Hallowe'en.

Most people stayed safe inside their houses with their doors tightly locked. But not Janna.

When all her household was fast asleep, out she crept again, into the darkness. She followed the path the cold moon showed her, a silver path that led straight back into the enchanted forest.

Somehow, Janna found her way back to the well.
And no sooner was she there than she heard noises.
Bells tinkled. Hooves thudded on the dewy grass.

Two huge black horses stepped out of the trees.
The Fairy King rode one, and beside him rode the Queen,
dazzling with a cold, unearthly beauty.

As Janna shrank away, the snow-white horse she had
seen the day before came whinnying into the clearing.
On its back was Tam Lin.

Janna hesitated. Then Tam Lin's grey eyes looked into hers and her heart melted. She rushed forward, took both his hands, and dragged him from the saddle.

The Queen gave a piercing shriek.

At once, an army of grim-faced fairies swarmed from the shadows. They leapt at Janna, cackling and cursing, poking and stabbing ...

Janna shut her eyes, gritted her teeth and held on to Tam Lin with all her might.

"So you love him, do you?" screamed the Fairy Queen.
"Are you sure? Look at him!"

Janna didn't want to, but she had to look. And she saw ...
Oh, it was horrible: the fairies had turned Tam Lin into
a slippery, writhing snake!

She closed her eyes again.

"Look!" shrieked the Queen. "Look at him now."

They had made him into a huge, roaring lion!

As Janna clung to its fur, it turned on her, slavering with hunger, showing its sharp yellow teeth ...

Then suddenly the lion was gone.

It had turned into a bar of red-hot metal. She clung to it, and her hands burned and blistered with a dreadful pain.

Janna staggered towards the well. If only she could dip her hands into the cool water, maybe the terrible pain would go.

As she reached the well's edge, the metal bar suddenly leapt from her hands of its own accord and splashed into the water. A great jet of steam gushed up into the cold night air. Silvery drops spattered everywhere.

Then everything went quiet.

"Thank you, my lady," said a voice.

Tam Lin was standing there, back in his own shape, so fine, strong and handsome. He was smiling, and the strange mists had gone from his eyes. He held out his hand, and this time Janna took it of her own free will.

They walked out of the forest together and back to Janna's house. All the way there they were talking, and soon they were laughing like old friends.

By the time they arrived, they had decided to get married. And so they did, and they loved each other deeply for the rest of their days.